Dear Parent:

Congratulations! Your child is taking the first steps on an exciting journey. The destination? Independent reading!

STEP INTO READING® will help your child get there. The program offers five steps to reading success. Each step includes fun stories and colorful art. There are also Step into Reading Sticker Books, Step into Reading Math Readers, Step into Reading Phonics Readers, Step into Reading Write-In Readers, and Step into Reading Phonics Boxed Sets—a complete literacy program with something for every child.

Learning to Read, Step by Step!

Ready to Read   Preschool–Kindergarten
• big type and easy words • rhyme and rhythm • picture clues
For children who know the alphabet and are eager to begin reading.

Reading with Help   Preschool–Grade 1
• basic vocabulary • short sentences • simple stories
For children who recognize familiar words and sound out new words with help.

Reading on Your Own   Grades 1–3
• engaging characters • easy-to-follow plots • popular topics
For children who are ready to read on their own.

Reading Paragraphs   Grades 2–3
• challenging vocabulary • short paragraphs • exciting stories
For newly independent readers who read simple sentences with confidence.

Ready for Chapters   Grades 2–4
• chapters • longer paragraphs • full-color art
For children who want to take the plunge into chapter books but still like colorful pictures.

STEP INTO READING® is designed to give every child a successful reading experience. The grade levels are only guides. Children can progress through the steps at their own speed, developing confidence in their reading, no matter what their grade.

Remember, a lifetime love of reading starts with a single step!

For Princess Emily, with love —C.B.C.

Visit us on the Web!
StepIntoReading.com
randomhouse.com/kids

Educators and librarians, for a variety of teaching tools, visit us at RHTeachersLibrarians.com

ISBN 978-0-7364-3155-2 (trade) — ISBN 978-0-7364-8158-8 (lib. bdg.)
Printed in the United States of America   10 9 8 7

STEP INTO READING®

STEP 2

Snuggle Buddies

Adapted by Courtney Carbone

Based on text by Amy Sky Koster

Illustrated by the Disney Storybook Art Team

Random House 🏠 New York

Pumpkin is
a playful puppy.
She cannot sit still!

She likes

to twirl and swirl.

Berry is a shy bunny.
She lives
in the woods.

She loves

to eat ripe berries.

They are so tasty!

Beauty is
a sleepy kitty.

She likes long naps.

Shh! Don't wake her up!

Blondie is a small pony
with a big wish.

She wants to be
a royal horse!
Will her dream
come true?

Pumpkin needs a home.

The Prince thinks she
would love the palace!
He thinks Cinderella
would love Pumpkin.

Berry is hungry.

She wants some berries.

Snow White has
a whole bucket
full of berries!

Aurora finds Beauty

asleep in her garden.

Beauty wakes up!

They share a smile.

Aurora loves

the pretty kitty!

Blondie sneaks

into the royal parade.

It is so much fun!

Rapunzel watches
the show.

Cinderella dances

the night away.

Pumpkin joins in!
What a big surprise
for Cinderella!
She watches the
dancing puppy.

Snow White has
baked a pie.
It is blueberry!
Berry's favorite!

Berry comes out
from her hiding place.
She was in the
bucket of berries!

Aurora has three
fairy friends.
They will help
take care of Beauty.

Aurora brings Beauty
to the palace.

Rapunzel spots
Blondie.

She knows
the pony is special!
The crowd cheers.

Cinderella and Pumpkin
dance together!

Berry is the perfect pet
for Snow White.

Aurora hugs

her sweet kitty.

Rapunzel makes Blondie
a royal horse!

The princesses have found snuggly palace pets!